CW00746185

HORSE HERO

Also in the Animal Ark Pets Series

Plus
Little Animal Ark 1–10
Animal Ark 1–56
Animal Ark Hauntings 1–9

LUCY DANIELS

Horse
Hero

Illustrated by Paul Howard

Hodder
Children's
Books

a division of Hodder Headline Limited

Special thanks to Narinder Dhami

Text copyright © 2002 Working Partners Limited,
Created by Working Partners Limited, London W6 0QT
Illustrations copyright © 2002 Paul Howard
Cover illustration by Chris Chapman

First published in Great Britain in 2002
by Hodder Children's Books

The right of Lucy Daniels to be identified as the Author of
this Work has been asserted by her in accordance with the
Copyright, Designs and Patents Act 1988.

10 9 8 7 6 5 4 3 2 1

All rights reserved. No part of this publication may be reproduced,
stored in a retrieval system, or transmitted, in any form or by any
means without the prior written permission of the publisher, nor be
otherwise circulated in any form of binding or cover other than that
in which it is published and without a similar condition being
imposed on the subsequent purchaser.

All characters in this publication are fictitious and any resemblance
to real persons, living or dead, is purely coincidental.

A Catalogue record for this book is available from
the British Library

ISBN 0 340 85204 6

Typeset by Avon Dataset Ltd, Bidford-on-Avon, Warks

Printed and bound in Great Britain by
The Guernsey Press Co. Ltd, Channel Isles

Hodder Children's Books
a division of Hodder Headline Limited
338 Euston Road
London NW1 3BH

Contents

Contents

1

A perfect partnership

"Oh!" cried Mandy Hope, clapping her hands over her ears. "That's loud!" The police siren blared out over the field behind Mrs Forsyth's riding stables. Mandy was watching a police horse demonstration with the rest of the Pony Club.

"Yes, but look at Marlow. He doesn't mind a bit," said Mandy's friend, Lucy Kaye. Lucy and her twin brother William were in Mandy's class at Welford Primary.

The big chestnut police horse was standing quietly in the middle of the field. Then his rider, PC Nick Greenall, urged the horse to walk forwards, straight towards the loudspeaker. Marlow's ears flicked to and fro as the noise got louder, but he still didn't seem to mind. He walked calmly towards the loudspeaker without turning a hair.

Mandy was really enjoying watching the police horse show off his skills. The demonstration had started with PC Greenall introducing Marlow to the members of the Pony Club, and telling them a bit about how police horses were trained. Then Marlow had begun to show them what he could do.

"Isn't Marlow brilliant?" Lucy said admiringly.

Mandy nodded. She loved horses. In fact, Mandy was animal-mad, and she often thought it was a very good thing that both of her parents were vets. Their surgery was built on to the back of their cottage in Welford. Mandy couldn't have a pet of her own because there was always so much

going on at Animal Ark, but she didn't really mind. She enjoyed meeting all the different animals who came into the surgery for treatment. And having friends in the Pony Club meant she got to see amazing horses like Marlow!

"You can see that our horses are trained to avoid loud noises!" PC Greenall called with a grin. He was a friendly young man with short red hair and twinkling blue eyes, and he looked very smart in his navy-blue police uniform. As Miss Fletcher turned off the loudspeaker, PC Greenall rode Marlow over to the fence, towards the watching crowd. "Police horses do a lot of work like controlling football crowds, for instance," PC Greenall went on, "and they're never very quiet! So we can't let our horses get spooked by loud noises."

"Has anyone got a question for PC Greenall?" asked Mrs Forsyth, looking round at the Pony Club members.

"I have," Lucy said shyly. "What kind of horses make the best police horses?"

"That's a very good question," the policeman replied. "A good police horse has to be strong and very even-tempered. They have to obey orders quickly. But a police horse shouldn't be *too* calm and quiet. They have to be brave and fearless, too."

"How long do you have to train to become a mounted police officer?" asked Lucy's twin brother, William. "And is the training difficult?"

PC Greenall smiled at him. "We train for almost six months," he replied. "And yes, it's quite hard. But it's worth it when you get your own horse."

Mandy put up her hand. "Are all the horses as big as Marlow?" she asked.

"Marlow's one of the bigger ones. He's nearly seventeen hands," PC Greenall told her. "But police horses can't be less than sixteen hands high."

Mandy leaned over the fence and stared up at Marlow. His smooth chestnut-coloured coat shone. Even his huge hooves were polished and gleaming. Marlow *was* big, Mandy thought, but his dark eyes were calm and friendly. He really was a gentle giant.

Marlow noticed Mandy watching him. He

bent his head down to look more closely at her, then blew gently on her hand.

"As I said before, most of our work involves crowd control," PC Greenall went on, "and if you're trying to control a large crowd, a big horse is very useful."

Mandy turned to Lucy and grinned. "Yes, a Shetland pony wouldn't be much good, would it?" she said.

Everyone burst out laughing, including PC Greenall.

"You're right," the policeman agreed. "A big horse is much safer. It means that when I'm on Marlow's back, I can see over the top of the crowd. And the crowd can see Marlow easily too. But a big horse can also cause problems if it's not properly trained. Why do you think that is?"

"Because he might squash someone in the crowd?" Mandy suggested.

"Exactly." PC Greenall nodded. "If Marlow is controlling a crowd of people, we might not have a lot of room to move about, so we have to train our horses to stay calm, whatever happens."

Mandy glanced at Marlow. She couldn't

imagine the big police horse *ever* getting into a panic. He looked so calm and wise.

"Let me show you some of the other things that Marlow can do," said PC Greenall. He nodded at two of the older Pony Club members. They immediately ran out on to the field, and spread a large plastic sheet on the grass. "We train our horses to be confident about walking on all kinds of surfaces," PC Greenall explained. "If a horse doesn't like the look of something, he'll step around it or jump over it, or even run away! We have to make sure our horses don't do that."

Mandy's friend, Paul Stevens, put up his hand. "That's just like my Exmoor pony, Paddy," he said with a grin. "He doesn't even like walking on shadows!"

"When horses feel they are in danger, their first thought is to run away," said PC Greenall. "So it's very important that there is a lot of trust between the horse and his rider. That gives the horse the courage to face difficult situations." PC Greenall leaned out of his saddle and patted Marlow's glossy chestnut neck. Mandy smiled. It was easy to see that Marlow and the policeman were best friends.

Marlow looked alert and interested as PC Greenall urged him forward, towards the plastic sheet. He didn't seem at all worried by this strange thing laid out on the grass. Neatly lifting his huge hooves, he trotted right across it, and stopped on the other side. Everyone clapped, and Marlow dipped his head and shook his mane, as if he was saying *Thank you!*

Everyone clapped again. Mandy was enjoying herself so much, she couldn't help wishing that her best friend James Hunter had come with her. But James had gone on holiday with his family for two weeks. Mandy had thought that James was lucky to be missing school, but now he was missing Marlow's demonstration too. She'd have to tell him all about it when he came home.

"This is something else we use in training," PC Greenall called out, as Mrs Forsyth pushed an enormous red rubber ball into the middle of the field. "We have to get the horses used to all kinds of strange obstacles! Some of the horses are scared of the ball at first, but we start off just by riding around it, like this."

Mandy watched as PC Greenall and Marlow circled the ball a few times.

"Then another officer sits on the ball, while the horses watch," PC Greenall continued. "That makes them think that maybe the ball isn't *quite* so dangerous! Then we start doing this."

Marlow walked towards the ball and pushed it forward with his chest. It rolled a short distance away from him. Marlow trotted after it and gave it another push, then another. He looked as if he was enjoying himself. Mandy and the rest of the Pony Club clapped loudly.

"Now, to finish off, I'd like to show you how good Marlow is at ignoring a noisy crowd." PC Greenall's eyes twinkled even more. "I hope you'll all volunteer!"

Mrs Forsyth opened the gate into the field and the Pony Club members streamed through, chattering excitedly to each other.

"Isn't this great?" Mandy said eagerly to Lucy and William. "We'll have to make lots of noise!"

"Marlow won't mind," said Lucy, her eyes still fixed on the handsome chestnut horse. "You know, I'd love to do PC Greenall's job when I grow up."

"What, be a mounted policeman?" Mandy asked, looking surprised. Lucy had never mentioned it before.

"No, a police*woman*, actually," Lucy said with a grin.

"You know what I mean!" Mandy laughed. "Maybe you could ask PC Greenall to give you some advice."

All the Pony Club members stood together in a crowd at one end of the field. Mrs Forsyth and Miss Fletcher, the Pony Club Secretary, walked round handing out whistles and flags.

"Here you are, Mandy," said Miss Fletcher with a smile, handing her an enormous flag on a long pole. "This is the biggest one, so make sure you wave it around as hard as you can!"

"Oh!" Mandy couldn't help gasping when she saw the huge red and white flag. Carefully she took it from Miss Fletcher. "It's really heavy."

"Don't wave it *too* hard, Mandy," William grinned, as Mandy waved the flag over her head a few times to try it out. "It's a windy day – you might take off!"

Marlow and PC Greenall were waiting on the other side of the field. "When I raise my hand, start making as much noise as you like," the police officer called.

Everyone waited for the signal, then they began to blow their whistles and wave their flags. The flags flapped wildly in the breeze, and the whistles screeched deafeningly. Mandy stood right at the front of the crowd with her giant flag and waved it as hard as she could.

Marlow trotted from one side of the field to the other, passing very close to the crowd. His ears twitched, but that was the only sign he gave of hearing any noise. The big horse brushed right past Mandy and her flag, but it didn't seem to worry him at all.

"Well done, Marlow!" Mandy called, resting the flagpole against her shoulder and clapping until her hands hurt.

Miss Fletcher stepped forward. "Thank you very much, PC Greenall and Marlow," she

said. "I know everyone has enjoyed the demonstration very much."

There was a loud murmur of agreement from all the Pony Club members.

"I can see that some of your parents are already arriving to collect you," Miss Fletcher went on, glancing over at the stables, "so off you go, and see you at our next meeting."

Mandy was pleased that she, Lucy and William didn't have to rush off immediately. After Marlow's demonstration, the twins had promised to show Mandy their new pony, Honey, who was stabled at the riding school. Mandy couldn't wait. Mrs Kaye had arranged to collect them a little later to give them plenty of time to spend with Honey. This meant that they also had time to go over and meet Marlow properly. He was standing patiently while PC Greenall chatted to Miss Fletcher.

"You were great, Marlow," Mandy said, stroking the horse's strong neck.

Marlow gave a gentle snort and tossed his silky mane.

"Did you enjoy the demonstration?" PC Greenall smiled at Mandy, Lucy and William.

"It was brilliant!" Lucy said eagerly, patting Marlow's shoulder. "I'd like to be a mounted policewoman when I grow up."

"Oh?" PC Greenall looked pleased. "It's a very interesting job. You have to love riding, but as you're a Pony Club member, I don't need to tell *you* that!"

Lucy didn't say anything, and Mandy noticed that her friend suddenly looked a bit upset, biting her lip and staring down at her riding-boots. Mandy wondered what the matter was.

"Bye, Marlow." William stroked the horse's nose. "I hope we see you again."

"Wasn't Marlow wonderful?" Lucy sighed, as they set off across the field towards the stables. "I'd love to ride a horse just like him when I'm a policewoman."

Mandy smiled. Lucy seemed fine now, and she had obviously fallen in love with the big police horse. Maybe Mandy had just been imagining things . . .

2

Lucy's secret

"Here she is," Lucy said proudly. She walked out of the stable leading a beautiful, honey-coloured pony with a long golden mane and big brown eyes. "Mandy, meet Honey. Honey, meet Mandy."

"Oh, she's gorgeous!" Mandy gasped.

"Isn't she great?" said William, sounding just as proud as his twin. "She's really quiet

15

and gentle, but she's ever so clever too."

Mandy ran her fingers across the pony's silky coat, loving the feel of it. Honey sniffed at Mandy's jacket, and then snuffled at one of the pockets, trying to get her nose inside.

Mandy began to laugh. "She's found my mints!" she said. Mandy always brought a packet of mints with her when she came to visit the stables.

"I told you she was clever, didn't I?" William grinned.

Mandy put a mint on the palm of her hand and held it out flat to Honey. The pony took it immediately, her tongue gently tickling Mandy's skin.

"Only one!" Mandy told her, as Honey began to nose around her pocket again. "Too many sweet things aren't good for you."

"Mum's going to be here soon." William glanced at his watch. "We won't have time to ride Honey if we don't hurry up."

Mandy saw that Lucy looked upset again. This time she was *sure* she wasn't imagining things. What was going on?

"Do you want to have first go on Honey,

Lucy?" William asked, staring hard at his sister. "I don't mind."

Mandy looked from one twin to the other. She couldn't understand why Lucy looked so miserable.

"No, you go first," Lucy mumbled.

William sighed. "OK, I'll tack Honey up," he said, and he led the pony away.

Mandy didn't know what to say. What on earth could be the matter with Lucy? "Honey's a lovely pony," she said at last.

"Yes, she is," Lucy agreed.

They stood there in silence.

"What's wrong, Lucy?" Mandy asked. "It's not Honey, is it?"

"Oh no!" Lucy said firmly. "I *love* Honey." She stared down at her boots for a moment. "It's me, Mandy," she blurted out. "I'm scared of riding."

"Oh, *Lucy*." Mandy was stunned. She could hardly believe what her friend had just told her. Lucy was *mad* about horses. She had been ever since Mandy had known the twins. William was the same. The Kayes even spent most of their holidays pony-trekking. It seemed impossible to Mandy that Lucy, of all people, would be scared of getting on a horse.

"What happened, Lucy?" Mandy prompted.

Lucy looked miserably at her. "It happened at half-term," she said. "You know, when Mum and Dad took us pony-trekking in Wales. We were just about to leave the stables, and – well, I fell off my pony."

"Didn't you get straight back on again?" Mandy asked. She knew that was supposed to be the best way to get over any nerves.

Lucy shook her head. "No, if I'd done

that, I might have been OK," she muttered. "But I hurt my ankle, so I couldn't ride for the rest of the holiday. And I haven't ridden since."

Mandy was amazed. It was near the end of the summer term, so half-term had been several weeks ago. If Lucy hadn't ridden for that long, it *must* be serious.

"Then Mum and Dad bought us Honey for our birthday," Lucy went on sadly. "I haven't even been able to ride her yet."

"Do your parents know?" Mandy asked. She felt very sorry for Lucy.

"No, only William knows," Lucy replied. "And you."

"Don't worry, Lucy," Mandy said comfortingly. "You used to love riding so much, I'm sure you'll start again soon."

"I know." Lucy brightened up at Mandy's words. "I think I just need a bit of time to get over the fall."

Mandy agreed with her. She couldn't imagine Lucy not getting on a horse again.

"We're all set!" William called. He was on Honey's back, trotting across the stable yard towards them.

Mandy saw a look of envy flash across Lucy's face. Lucy really did want to start riding again, Mandy thought. That was a good sign.

"William, did you check Honey's back leg?" Lucy asked anxiously, as her brother brought the pony to a halt. "You know it was a bit swollen yesterday."

"No, I forgot," William admitted.

Lucy bent down and ran her hand over one of Honey's hind legs. "It's fine now, I think," she said. She turned to Mandy. "We were going to ask your mum or dad to come and check Honey over if it got worse," she explained.

Mandy watched as Honey nudged her head lovingly against Lucy's shoulder. Although

Lucy had never ridden Honey, the two of them seemed to be very close.

William urged Honey to walk on, and the pony obeyed immediately. Mandy and Lucy followed them towards the field. Once they were inside, Honey broke into a trot, then she and William cantered briskly round the field.

Mandy glanced sideways at Lucy as they leaned over the fence, watching. She could tell that Lucy really wished that *she* was the one riding their new pony.

There was no point in worrying about it too much, Mandy thought. When Lucy was ready to get back into the saddle, it would happen. Mandy was sure of it.

3

The Pony Club Show

"Hello, you two." Mrs Kaye, the twins' mother, walked across the stable yard, waving at Mandy and Lucy. William and Honey were still trotting round the field. "How was the police horse display?"

"Oh, Mum, it was great," Lucy said eagerly. "Marlow could do so many things, and nothing frightened him. Not even a really loud siren."

"We had to pretend to be a noisy crowd," Mandy added. "I had the biggest flag, and I had to wave it right under Marlow's nose!"

"It sounds like great fun," said Mrs Kaye, then she glanced at her watch. "I'm a little earlier than I said I would be," she went on. "I forgot that there's a Women's Institute meeting tonight." She looked at Lucy. "Have you had a ride on Honey yet, love?"

Lucy turned bright pink. Mandy felt very sorry for her. "I don't mind missing my turn if you're in a hurry, Mum," Lucy muttered.

"Well, if you're sure . . ." replied Mrs Kaye. Lucy's mum didn't seem to suspect that anything was wrong.

"Oh, *Mum*!" William groaned, riding Honey over to the fence. "You're loads earlier than you said you would be. I've hardly had a go on Honey at all."

"Sorry, dear, I forgot I had a meeting to go to this evening," Mrs Kaye replied. "Go on, have five more minutes. We've still got a bit of time."

"Don't forget we have to rub Honey down

and give her some pony nuts before we go," Lucy reminded her brother.

"Why don't *you* ride Honey for the last five minutes, Lucy?" William looked at his sister. "Go on."

Mandy's heart began to thump. What would Lucy say?

"No, it's OK," Lucy mumbled, staring down at her feet. "I'll have to adjust the stirrups and everything because I'm taller than you. We don't have that much time. You keep going, William."

Mandy thought that William was about to argue, but in the end he didn't. Instead he and Honey trotted off across the field. Mandy knew that William was only trying to help his twin, but she wondered if it might be better to leave Lucy alone and let her decide for herself when she wanted to ride again. Mandy decided to talk to her mum and dad about it, and ask them what they thought.

After another five minutes, William reluctantly led Honey back into the stable yard. Lucy and Mandy were waiting with the currycomb and the brushes, ready to

groom Honey and get her settled in her stable for the night. Honey stood patiently as they took off her tack and brushed out the saddle marks.

"There you are, Honey." Lucy put a pale blue cotton sheet over the pony's back and led her into the stable. "We'll see you soon." And she planted a kiss on Honey's nose.

"Are you three still here?" Miss Fletcher came out of the Pony Club office, carrying a piece of paper in her hand. "Oh, hello, Mrs Kaye."

"Hello, Miss Fletcher. Actually, we're just going." The twins' mum glanced at her watch again. "Come on then, you three, or I'm going to be late for my meeting."

"Before you go, you might be interested in this." Miss Fletcher pinned the piece of paper to the stables' noticeboard. "I meant to put it up earlier, but with all the excitement over Marlow and PC Greenall, I completely forgot. It's about this year's Pony Club Show." The Pony Club Show was part of the Welford Show, which took place in a field at the edge of the village every year.

Mandy, Lucy and William crowded round the noticeboard.

"Can we enter Honey, Mum?" William asked eagerly, as he ran his finger down the piece of paper. "Look, there's loads of different classes. Junior Jumping, Fancy Dress Jumping, Handy Pony . . ."

"Handy Pony?" Lucy frowned, and looked at Mandy. "What's that?"

"I don't know," Mandy admitted. "What is it, Miss Fletcher?"

"Well, the ponies have to do things like ignore strange noises and walk on plastic sheets," Miss Fletcher explained. "I have a list in the office of all the things they're required to do." She smiled at them. "The Handy Pony is a good class for really calm, steady ponies who aren't easily frightened."

Mandy turned to Lucy. "That sounds like the kind of stuff Marlow does!" she exclaimed.

"Yes." Lucy's eyes were shining. "It would be fun to teach Honey to do the same things as Marlow."

"Mum, can we enter Honey in *all* of these classes?" William demanded, looking very excited. "She's so clever, she'd win them all! I know she would."

Mrs Kaye and Miss Fletcher laughed.

"I don't think so, William," his mum replied. "Poor Honey would be tired out."

"And anyway, some of the classes are for the older members of the club only," Miss Fletcher added.

William looked disappointed.

"You and Lucy can enter Honey in one class each," Mrs Kaye said firmly. "Which ones are you going to choose?"

Mandy looked at Lucy. The Welford Show was in a few weeks' time. Would Lucy be riding Honey by then? From the look on Lucy's face, she was thinking exactly the same thing.

"I think I'll enter the Junior Jumping class," William decided. "Honey's done some jumping before, so she should be really good."

"And what about you, Lucy?" Mrs Kaye asked. "Which class do *you* want to enter?"

Mandy held her breath.

"I think I *might* enter the Handy Pony class," Lucy said bravely.

"Good idea," William beamed.

"But first we'll have to train Honey to do those things Miss Fletcher mentioned," Lucy added quickly. "So it all depends on how well Honey does. She might not be good enough to enter the competition."

"I'm sure she will be," William said confidently. "We'll start training her tomorrow."

"I think the Handy Pony class is a great idea," Mandy said to Lucy, as they all walked over to Mrs Kaye's car. "You can train Honey to be just like Marlow!"

"Yes, I hope so," Lucy said uncertainly. "You'll help us, won't you, Mandy?"

"Of course I will," Mandy said. She really hoped that Lucy and Honey would be taking part in the Handy Pony competition. But they would just have to wait and see.

4

The training begins

"So did you enjoy the police horse demonstration, Mandy?" asked Adam Hope, pouring himself a cup of tea.

Mandy nodded. It was the following morning, and the Hopes were having breakfast. Mandy had hurried home the previous evening, longing to tell her parents all about Marlow, but both her parents had been called out to emergencies. Mr Hope was treating a sick sheep at one of the local farms, and Mrs Hope had gone to examine a dog who'd been knocked down by a car. So Mandy had got home to find her grandparents, who also lived in Welford, waiting for her. Mandy was a bit disappointed, but she was used to her parents rushing out on emergency calls. And, luckily, her mum and dad had told Mandy that both the dog and the sheep were going to be fine.

"Oh, Dad, Marlow's so clever," Mandy said eagerly. "Nothing seems to worry him at all." And she described how the police horse had

completely ignored the noisy crowd and the flapping flags.

"Those police horses are pretty special," remarked Emily Hope, pushing her red hair out of her eyes. "They're very highly trained indeed."

"Lucy thought Marlow was great too," Mandy said, spreading butter on her toast. "She wants to be a mounted policewoman when she grows up."

"Well, she's certainly horse-mad!" Mandy's mum laughed. "That always helps."

"Yes," Mandy said. But she couldn't help sighing, when she remembered Lucy's problem.

Mrs Hope glanced at Mandy. "That was a big sigh, love," she said gently. "What's the matter?"

"Lucy told me yesterday that she's scared of riding," Mandy explained. "She hasn't ridden for ages."

Mandy's mum looked surprised. "Lucy, scared of riding?"

"How did that happen?" asked Mr Hope.

Mandy explained how Lucy had fallen off a pony on holiday. "The Pony Club Show's coming up in a few weeks' time," she went on, "and Lucy wants to enter Honey in the Handy Pony class. But she doesn't know if she'll be able to ride her."

"Is Lucy just scared of riding?" Mrs Hope asked. "Or she is frightened of horses in general?"

"Oh no," Mandy said firmly. "Lucy's not frightened of horses at all. She's *brilliant* with Honey. Even better than William is, really. And she loved Marlow."

"Well, that's a good sign," said Mr Hope.

"Is there anything Lucy can do to help her get over her fear of riding?" Mandy asked, looking from her mum to her dad.

"It's down to Lucy herself, I'm afraid," Mrs Hope replied. "It's no good trying to force her."

"Don't worry, Mandy," her dad said comfortingly. "The Pony Club Show may be just the boost that Lucy needs to get her back in the saddle."

"Is William entering any classes?" Mandy's mum asked.

"Yes, the Junior Jumping." Mandy grinned at her parents. "He wanted to enter Honey in *all* the classes but his mum and Miss Fletcher wouldn't let him!"

"He likes to win, doesn't he?" Mr Hope laughed. "Do you remember the egg and spoon race at your school Sports Day? William dropped his own egg, and picked up someone else's so that he could win!"

Mandy laughed. "Yes, and he was really annoyed when he was disqualified," she added.

"Just don't be too surprised if Lucy decides she can't go through with riding at the show, Mandy," her mum pointed out gently. "I'm sure Lucy will start riding again soon, but it might not be for a while yet."

"OK," Mandy said. "I understand. Did I tell you that Lucy and William want me to help them to train Honey?"

"Do they?" Mr Hope picked up his Sunday newspaper and unfolded it. "That sounds like fun."

"I know," Mandy agreed. "They've asked me to go over to the stables this morning so that we can make a start."

Mr Hope rolled his eyes. "I suppose you want a lift over there?" he said with a smile.

"Yes please, Dad," Mandy said eagerly. "But first I've got to finish making my washing-line."

Mr Hope raised his eyebrows at her. "Your washing-line?"

"That's right!" Mandy laughed. She went over to the corner of the kitchen and picked up a black rubbish sack. She opened it up and pulled out a long clothes line. There were lots of clothes pegged to it. "It's for the Handy Pony competition. The ponies have to walk underneath a washing-line full of clothes. We're going to practise that today."

"I hope you haven't used any of *your* clothes, Mandy!" her mum exclaimed, looking closely at the washing-line.

"Gran lent the clothes to me," Mandy said quickly. "They're part of the things she's collected for the next WI jumble sale. When I told her and Grandad about the Handy Pony competition last night, she popped back to Lilac Cottage and got them for me."

Emily Hope looked relieved. "In that case, I think it's a great practice washing-line!" she laughed.

Mandy fetched some more pegs, and carried

on pegging the old clothes to the washing-line. She couldn't *wait* to start Honey's training. She was sure the gentle little pony was going to do really well.

When Mandy and Mr Hope arrived at the stables, Lucy and William were already out in the paddock with Honey. They were talking to a couple of the helpers and pointing to some bales of straw which were stacked in a corner of the field.

"Thanks, Dad." Mandy scrambled quickly out of the Land-rover, carrying the black sack with the washing-line in it. "I'll see you later."

"Good luck with the training!" Mr Hope called, waving at Mandy. "And I'll keep my fingers crossed for Lucy."

Mandy set off towards the paddock.

Lucy saw her coming and ran over to meet her. She had a piece of paper in her hand. "Hi, Mandy," she called. "We only got here a few minutes ago, so we haven't started yet. Look." She held out the piece of paper. "Miss Fletcher gave me this list of the things Honey has to do for the Handy Pony competition."

Mandy read the list. Apart from the things they already knew about, such as walking under a line of washing, there were several others – like weaving in and out of poles and carrying a small sack of straw between two cones.

"What do you think, Mandy?" Lucy asked eagerly. "I'm sure that Honey will be able to do all these things easily. She's *so* clever."

"Of course she will!" Mandy said.

"Anyway," Lucy sighed, looking a bit miserable again, "it's not Honey who's the problem – it's me."

"You and Honey can have fun training whether you take part in the competition or not," Mandy pointed out. "And even if you don't enter this year, there's always *next* year."

Lucy brightened up again. "Yes, you're right," she agreed. "Come on, we're going to stack up the bales of straw and teach Honey how to walk between them. William's going to ride her."

"OK," Mandy said. "And I've made a washing-line full of clothes."

They hurried across the field. William and the helpers were dragging the bales of straw into position, leaving a narrow path in the middle for Honey to walk through.

"Don't make it too long to start with," Lucy called. "Honey might be scared until she's got used to it."

As soon as the bales of straw had been stacked, William went over to Honey, who was waiting patiently, tied to the fence. "Come on, Honey," he said, as he fitted his foot into the stirrup. "This is easy. I know you can do it."

"No, wait, William," said Lucy. "I think we should *lead* Honey through the bales first, not *ride* her." She put her hand in her pocket and pulled out a roll of mints. "And these are to give her when she's done it."

"That's a great idea, Lucy," Mandy said. It was always a good idea to reward animals with a treat when you were trying to teach them something new.

"OK," William agreed. "Do you want to lead Honey then, Lucy?"

"Yes, of course," said Lucy, her face lighting up.

Mandy watched as Lucy went over to Honey. At first she just stroked the pony's nose and talked to her in a low voice for a moment. Then she untied the rope and led Honey over to the bales of straw.

Lucy stood patiently at the entrance to the narrow path between the bales, waiting for Honey to feel comfortable before they moved forward. When Honey stopped and pulled backwards slightly, Lucy stopped too. She didn't try to force Honey to walk on until the pony was ready, and she talked softly to Honey all the time. Soon the pony was on the move again, and a moment later they'd reached the end of the path.

"Well done, Honey!" Lucy said proudly, giving the pony a mint. Honey munched it

happily, and looked quite proud of herself too.

"Well done, *Lucy*!" Mandy said with a grin. "You were both great."

"Shall we try again?" Lucy asked.

This time Honey didn't seem nervous at all. She followed Lucy calmly through the narrow gap, and then nudged her for another mint.

"Brilliant!" William shouted excitedly. "Now let's try using a few more bales."

They hauled some more bales of straw into position, and made the path longer. Once again Lucy led Honey through the gap without any problems.

"I think I should try riding Honey now," William said. "Maybe you'd better still lead her though, Lucy."

Finally, William rode between the bales without Lucy leading the pony. Mandy and Lucy watched closely, but Honey showed no signs at all of being nervous or scared. Mandy grinned to herself. It looked like they'd managed to teach Honey her very first Handy Pony skill!

"You were brilliant, Honey!" cried Lucy,

rushing over to throw her arms around the pony's neck. "I don't think even Marlow could have done it better."

"Honey, you're going to be the Handiest Pony ever!" Mandy laughed. She glanced at Lucy's shining eyes and proud face. Mandy was sure that Honey and Lucy had a good chance of winning the Handy Pony competition. It was a great start.

5

An unexpected problem

"So how is Honey coming along?" asked Mrs Kaye, as she drove along the road to the stables. "Is she going to do well in the Handy Pony competition?"

"*Really* well!" said Lucy, William and Mandy together.

It was the following Saturday. Mandy had been at the stables almost every evening after

school that week to help Lucy and William train Honey. Things were going better than any of them had expected. Honey was proving very easy to train, and they'd already taught her several of the skills she would need for the Handy Pony class. The night before, they'd practised carrying a flag around. The rider had to pick up a large flag on a long pole, walk along with it, and then stick it in a traffic cone.

Honey had been a bit worried at first by the flag flapping about in the breeze, but she'd soon got the hang of it. They'd also made lots of noise blowing whistles, which Honey had to ignore. By the end of the training session, Honey had learned to stand perfectly still when she heard a loud noise. Meanwhile, William had also been practising jumping with Honey on the evenings when they weren't training her for the Handy Pony.

"How's the jumping practice going, William?" Mandy asked.

"Oh, very well, thanks," William said with a big grin. "I went to Mrs Forsyth's junior jumping class on Tuesday night, and she said we were pretty good."

"It sounds like both of you might do quite well at the Welford Show," Mrs Kaye remarked as she turned into the stables.

"We're going to win," William boasted.

Lucy didn't say anything, but looked out of the car window across the yard.

Honey was watching out for them. She dipped her head and swished her tail to and fro, saying hello.

"What are we going to do today?" Mandy asked, as Lucy led the pony out of her stable and started to put on the saddle and bridle.

"I think we should practise the loud noises again," Lucy suggested. "Just to make sure Honey remembers what to do. I've brought the whistles."

"And then I think we should walk Honey over the plastic sheet," William added. "We haven't tried that yet."

Mandy rubbed Honey's nose. "I bet you'll be just fine," she told the pony.

They went into the paddock, and William mounted Honey. Meanwhile, Lucy and Mandy stood to one side, holding their whistles. As William urged Honey forward, they blew the whistles as hard as they could, then shouted at the tops of their voices. Honey's ears pricked up a little, but she didn't shy away. Instead she trotted right past Mandy and Lucy.

"That was great," said Lucy, as they gathered round to stroke Honey. "She's definitely OK with the whistles now."

"Right, let's get the plastic sheet then." William was keen to get started on something new. "Mrs Forsyth said she had one we could borrow."

William went off to ask Mrs Forsyth for the sheet, while Lucy and Mandy waited with Honey.

"She's doing well, isn't she?" Lucy observed proudly, patting the pony's warm neck.

"Yes, she is," Mandy replied. "But she can't go into this competition on her own, you know." She glanced over at her friend.

"I really *do* want to ride again, Mandy," Lucy muttered, burying her face in Honey's silky mane. "But it's just so *hard*."

Just then William came back, carrying a blue plastic sheet.

"It's really big, isn't it?" Mandy remarked, as they spread it out in the middle of the field. The plastic rippled and shimmered in the sunlight. "Maybe we should lead Honey across it first before William rides her."

"Yes, good idea," agreed Lucy, taking Honey's reins in her hand.

Mandy and William watched as Lucy led Honey towards the sheet of plastic. Then, all of a sudden, the pony panicked. One moment Honey was walking calmly towards the plastic, the next she reared up and shied away with a whinny of fear. Lucy was taken by surprise and she only just managed to hang on to Honey's reins.

Mandy and William ran over to them. Lucy was talking to the pony in a quiet, soothing voice, and stroking her nose. After a few moments, Honey stopped trembling and seemed to calm down.

"What happened?" William was shocked.

"Something scared Honey," Mandy said, staring down at the plastic sheet.

"Let's try again," Lucy suggested.

Mandy and William watched closely as

Lucy led Honey towards the plastic sheet once more. Even though Lucy moved very slowly and talked to Honey the whole time, Honey still objected to the sheet. Although she didn't rear up this time, she stuck her hooves into the grass and refused to budge.

"What's the matter with you, Honey?" William asked crossly.

"I don't know," Lucy replied. "But I don't want to force her."

"Honey's not happy at all." Mandy stared at the pony, who was hanging her head, looking miserable. "I think we should leave it for today."

William didn't look very happy either. Without saying a word, he stomped off towards the stables.

"He'll get over it," Lucy sighed. "I'm more worried about Honey. I thought she'd be as good as Marlow at this. Remember how he walked across the plastic sheet at the demonstration?"

Mandy nodded, thinking hard. "Maybe Honey's had some sort of problem with plastic sheets before," she suggested. "Maybe that's why she's scared of it."

"Oh!" Lucy suddenly clapped her hand over her mouth.

"What?" Mandy asked.

"This sounds a bit silly," Lucy began, "but I *have* noticed that Honey's scared of puddles."

Mandy looked puzzled.

"Honey always walks around puddles, never through them," Lucy explained. "Especially if the water's a bit muddy. Maybe Honey thinks the plastic sheet is a giant puddle."

"Perhaps," Mandy said thoughtfully.

"But what can we do about it?" asked Lucy. "If Honey can't do this, we've got no chance of winning the Handy Pony competition."

Mandy knew that Lucy was right. What were they going to do?

6

Marlow in trouble

No one had had any bright ideas by the time
Mrs Kaye turned up to take them home.
Mandy was feeling very sorry for Honey. The
pony had obviously been very distressed, and
that had upset Lucy. And Mandy could see
that William was a bit embarrassed about the
way he'd lost his temper. They were all feeling
quite depressed.

"Goodness me, what long faces!" Mrs Kaye remarked, as Mandy, Lucy and William climbed into the car. "What's happened?"

"Honey's training session didn't go very well," muttered William, reaching for his seat belt.

"Oh?" Mrs Kaye turned the car round and drove out of the stables. "Is it something you can put right?"

"We don't know," Lucy replied gloomily.

They drove to the Hopes' cottage in silence. When Mrs Kaye pulled up outside, Mandy turned to Lucy. "Shall I ask my dad about Honey?" she offered. "My mum's out today, but he might have some ideas."

"That's a really good idea, Mandy," Lucy said eagerly. "We'll see you tomorrow."

Mandy said her goodbyes, and climbed out of the car. She really hoped her dad would be able to help. As she opened the front door, she heard the phone ringing in the hall. Her dad sprinted out of the kitchen and picked it up. He nodded and smiled at Mandy. "Hello?" he said into the receiver. "Oh, hello, PC Greenall."

Mandy's ears immediately pricked up.

PC Greenall! Why was *he* ringing?

"Right, I see." Adam Hope listened closely to what PC Greenall was saying. "No, of course I don't mind coming to see him. I'll be with you very shortly."

"Dad," Mandy said breathlessly, as her father put the phone down, "is there something wrong with Marlow?"

"I'm afraid so," replied Mr Hope. "He was taking some football fans back to the station after a match, and he slipped on some wet cobbles. Apparently his front fetlock joint is very swollen." He grabbed his bag from the hall table. "The police vet is on holiday, so PC Greenall called me instead."

"Can I come with you, Dad?" Mandy pleaded.

Mr Hope nodded, and they hurried out to the Land-rover.

"Poor Marlow," Mandy said anxiously. "I hope he's going to be OK."

"We'll soon find out," Mr Hope replied, as he started the engine.

The police barracks were on the other side of Walton, a large town not far from Welford. The man on duty at the gate directed Mr

Hope and Mandy to the stables, where PC Greenall was waiting for them. He looked worried. "Thanks for coming," he said, shaking Adam Hope's hand. Then he noticed Mandy. "Hello." PC Greenall looked puzzled. "Haven't we met somewhere before?"

"Yes, at Welford Pony Club a few weeks ago," Mandy explained. "I was the one waving the biggest flag! I'm Mandy Hope."

"Ah, yes, I remember," said PC Greenall, as he led them over to Marlow's stable. "You were with the girl who wants to be a mounted policewoman."

"That's Lucy," Mandy said.

Marlow was looking rather sorry for himself. Mandy could see that there was a swelling at the bottom of one of his front legs. She watched as her father knelt down and ran his hand over the fetlock joint.

"Yes, there's quite a lot of swelling there," Mr Hope said.

"Oh, poor Marlow," Mandy said. She leaned over and rubbed Marlow's nose gently. He sniffed her hand and snorted warmly.

"But it's not too serious?" PC Greenall asked anxiously. Mandy guessed that a bad injury could mean Marlow would have to give up his job as a police horse. No wonder PC Greenall looked so worried.

"He'll be fine, but he'll need a few days of complete rest," replied Mr Hope. He opened his bag. "I'll just give him a pain-killing injection."

While Mr Hope treated Marlow, PC Greenall took Mandy outside to give her a tour of the stables. Most of the horses were out on duty, but a few were still in their boxes.

"I really enjoyed Marlow's demonstration," Mandy told PC Greenall, as she patted a grey horse called Pilot. "We're trying to train Lucy and William's pony to do some of the things Marlow did."

"Oh?" PC Greenall looked interested, so Mandy told him about the things they were doing to get Honey ready for the Handy Pony competition.

"It sounds like you're doing very well," the policeman remarked. "That's how we train our horses – we start in a small way, and then build up. It's no use trying to rush the horse too quickly into doing something new." He smiled at Mandy. "The horse has to feel comfortable at every single moment, otherwise it won't work."

"Yes," Mandy agreed, sighing as she remembered the problem they'd had with Honey that afternoon. "But what if the horse is scared of something, and you don't know why?"

"Like what?" asked PC Greenall.

"Well, we tried walking Honey over a plastic sheet," Mandy explained, "and she just wouldn't do it. She seemed really frightened.

Lucy thinks it might have something to do with Honey being scared of puddles."

"Hmm, that's interesting," PC Greenall said, stroking his chin. "If a horse or a pony is scared of something, it's usually because of something that's happened to them before. Lucy could be right – Honey might be scared of the plastic sheet because she thinks it's a puddle."

"So if we could find out why Honey's frightened of puddles, that might help," Mandy said.

"It might," the policeman agreed. "Anyway, don't give up," he went on. "Actually, I can tell you something which you might find helpful—"

But before PC Greenall could finish, Mandy's dad came out of Marlow's box. "He's going to be fine," he said. "But the leg will need hosing with cold water three times a day, to bring the swelling down."

"Thanks very much," PC Greenall said gratefully.

Just then another policeman hurried over to them. "Nick, the Superintendent wants a word," he said. "It's urgent."

"Sorry, I've got to go." PC Greenall smiled at Mandy, then shook Adam Hope's hand.

"Come on, Mandy," said her father, walking over to the Land-rover. Mandy followed him reluctantly. It was a pity PC Greenall hadn't had time to finish what he was saying, she thought. The policeman might have been about to tell her something that would help Honey . . .

7

A clue from the past

"Dad," Mandy began, as her father pulled away from the police barracks, "you know we've been training Honey?" Maybe her dad would be able to help instead.

Mr Hope nodded.

"Well, everything's been going really well," Mandy went on. "Then this afternoon we had a real problem." And she explained what had happened with the plastic sheet. "So Lucy thinks it might be because Honey's scared of puddles," Mandy finished.

Mr Hope frowned. "Do you know the name of Honey's previous owners?" he asked.

"Yes, Lucy told me." Mandy wondered why her dad was asking. "It was a girl called Emma Kirby."

"The Kirbys! That's it!" Mandy's dad said triumphantly. "They live in Walton, don't they?"

"I think so," Mandy replied.

"Well, I remember treating Honey when they owned her," Adam Hope went on. "They asked me to go and check her over, because there was something wrong with one of her hooves."

"What was the matter?" Mandy was hanging on her dad's every word.

"Emma told me that Honey had stepped on a sharp nail." Mr Hope glanced sideways at Mandy. "The nail was hidden in a muddy puddle, and that's why Honey didn't see it."

"So *that's* why Honey's scared of puddles!" Mandy exclaimed. "Oh, poor Honey."

Her father nodded. "She was in a lot of pain, and she took quite a long time to get better," he explained.

"And that's why she's scared of the plastic sheet," Mandy said, "because she thinks it's a puddle."

"Mystery solved," said Mr Hope.

"Dad, can we stop at the Kayes' house on the way home?" Mandy asked as they reached Welford. "I really want to tell Lucy and William about Honey."

"All right," her dad agreed.

Mandy's heart was thumping as they drew up outside the Kayes' house. She couldn't wait to tell Lucy and William what she'd found out about Honey. Now that they knew what she was scared of, they might be able to cure her fear.

Lucy opened the front door. She looked very surprised to see Mandy and Mr Hope standing on the doorstep. "Mandy! What are you doing here?" she asked.

William came out of the living-room to see what was going on.

Mandy grinned at both of them. "I think I've found out what Honey's frightened of,"

she said, and straight away she told them all about Honey injuring her hoof on the nail in the puddle.

Lucy looked very upset when Mandy had finished. "Oh, poor Honey!" she gasped. "She must have been really scared when we tried to make her walk across the sheet."

William looked miserably down at his shoes. "I wish I hadn't got so cross with her," he mumbled.

"Well, now that we know, we can be especially kind to her," Mandy told them. "And we can take the training really slowly. That's what PC Greenall told me to do."

"When did he tell you that?" Lucy asked, looking puzzled.

Mandy explained about their visit to see Marlow.

"Is he going to be all right?" Lucy said anxiously.

"He's going to be fine," Mr Hope told her.

"Oh, thank goodness," Lucy said, sounding relieved.

"So we can start again with Honey tomorrow," said William.

"Maybe we should leave the plastic sheet for a day or two," suggested Lucy, "just to give Honey a break. We can always come back to it later."

"That's a good idea," Mandy agreed. "There's plenty of other things we can practise."

"We've taught Honey just about everything on this list now," Lucy said, looking at the piece of paper. "Except for walking across the plastic sheet."

Mandy nodded. It was time to try that again.

It was Saturday afternoon, one week later, and Mandy, Lucy and William were in the paddock with Honey. They had carried on training Honey for the show, but they'd decided to forget about the plastic sheet for a while. Honey had started enjoying her training again, and things were going well.

"I think we should practise that Round the World thing first," said Lucy, smiling at her brother. "William nearly tied his legs in knots last time!"

Mandy and William both laughed. Round the World meant that the pony had to stand still while the rider turned all the way round in the saddle, swinging one leg over at a time.

"It's not as easy as it looks, you know," William complained. "Anyway, *I'm* not entering the Handy Pony competition, am I? You should be doing this, Lucy."

"I *have* been practising Round the World," Lucy retorted. She pointed at the gate on the other side of the field. "I've been sitting on the gate, pretending it's a horse!"

Mandy couldn't help laughing, and neither could William.

"You're going to have to ride Honey sometime though, Lucy," William pointed out. "Or you won't be taking part in the Handy Pony class at all."

Lucy's face fell.

"There's still a week to go before the show," Mandy reminded them quickly. "Come on, shall we get started?"

William mounted Honey and started practising the Round the World move. Mandy had suggested tying a piece of string to one of his riding boots so that he could remember which leg to move first. That made it easier.

Then they tried the other thing they'd taught Honey yesterday. She had to stand quietly while the rider picked up a bell off a barrel and rang it loudly. Then the bell had to be replaced carefully. If it fell off the barrel, the rider lost points. Honey was used to ignoring loud noises by now, so it had been easy to show her what to do.

"You were brilliant, Honey." Lucy patted her pony on the neck, then she turned to the others. "Shall we get the plastic sheet now?"

William dismounted and went over to his jacket. He'd put it down on the grass and hidden the plastic sheet underneath it so that Honey didn't spot it.

"Maybe we shouldn't unfold it," Mandy suggested, as William was about to shake the sheet open. "Remember what PC Greenall said about starting small, and building up."

"OK," William agreed. He tried to fold the plastic sheet into an even smaller square.

"It's still quite big, isn't it?" Lucy said in a worried voice. She glanced over at Honey, but the pony was too busy munching some grass to notice what was going on.

William put the folded sheet down on the grass and Lucy began to lead Honey towards it. It was quite a breezy day, and suddenly the wind lifted the plastic sheet so that one side flapped up. Honey whinnied with fright, and tried to jerk the reins from Lucy's hand.

"Ssh, Honey," Lucy soothed her quietly. "It's all right."

"We could hold the edges down with stones," Mandy said. So she and William hurried off round the field looking for stones, which they laid carefully on the plastic.

"Come on, Honey," Lucy said softly, and urged the pony forward again. But as soon as Honey spotted the plastic square in front of her, she shied away.

"This doesn't look like it's going to work." William sounded very disappointed. "Shall we keep on trying?"

"I don't think we should," said Lucy, looking upset. "Honey's just getting more and more frightened."

"But what about the Handy Pony competition?" asked William.

"We won't be able to take part, that's all," Lucy muttered, biting her lip unhappily. "I probably wouldn't have been able to ride her, anyway."

Mandy could see that Lucy was just as disappointed as William. They had all worked so hard at training Honey. What were they going to do?

"Hello there!"

A shout from behind them made Mandy

turn round. Her eyes opened wide in surprise. "It's PC Greenall," she gasped. "And Marlow!"

8

Some excellent advice

Mandy, Lucy and William dashed over to the gate. Mandy opened it, and PC Greenall and Marlow trotted through. The big chestnut horse looked healthy and full of life again. His eyes were bright and his coat was gleaming.

"Marlow looks much better, PC Greenall," Mandy said, patting the horse's broad neck.

Marlow swished his tail proudly and nuzzled Mandy's shoulder.

"Yes, his leg injury soon cleared up with the treatment your father suggested," PC Greenall said cheerfully.

"What are you doing here, PC Greenall?" asked Lucy. She stared adoringly up at Marlow.

"Well, today was our first day back on duty," replied the policeman. "There was a protest march in York, and we were there to keep an eye on the crowd." He grinned. "But it was all very peaceful, so there wasn't much for us to do. And I needed to have a word with Mrs Forsyth about something, so that's why we're here. I thought I'd let Marlow out of the horsebox and let him stretch his legs round the village."

"It's great to see you again, Marlow," Lucy beamed.

PC Greenall noticed Honey tied to the fence. "Is that your pony?" he asked.

"Yes, this is Honey," said Lucy. She untied Honey and led her over. Marlow and Honey seemed very interested in each other. They touched noses, then rubbed their heads together.

"She's a lovely pony," said PC Greenall, bending over to stroke Honey's head. "How's the training going, by the way? Mandy told me all about it."

"Not very well," Lucy sighed. "Honey is still really scared of the plastic sheet."

"We found out why, though," Mandy said, and she told PC Greenall all about the nail in the puddle.

"Well, that certainly explains Honey's reaction," PC Greenall remarked, when Mandy had finished. "Horses are very careful about where they put their feet. Having healthy hooves is very important to them because when they're in danger, they need to be able to run away quickly."

"PC Greenall, when I was at the police horse stables you said you had something to tell me," Mandy said eagerly. "What was it?"

"That's right!" said PC Greenall. "I remember now." He jumped off Marlow's back, and grinned at them. "What would you say if I told you that *Marlow* nearly didn't make it as a police horse, because he had the very same problem as Honey? He wouldn't go near the sheet!"

"What?" Mandy gasped. She couldn't believe her ears.

"Not *Marlow*?" said Lucy, sounding shocked.

PC Greenall nodded. "Yes," he said. "I didn't know why Marlow was so scared of the plastic sheet, but he was. Perhaps there was a reason for it, like Honey, but he just wouldn't put a single hoof on that plastic."

"So what did you do?" Mandy asked.

"Well, we started with a very small strip, about this wide." PC Greenall held his hands about ten centimetres apart. "Marlow didn't seem to mind that. Then we moved on to wider strips. And each time he walked across the strips, I gave him a treat."

"We could do that," said Lucy. "I've brought some apples for Honey."

"I'll go and ask Mrs Forsyth for some scissors to cut the plastic into strips," yelled William, dashing off.

"Make sure Mrs Forsyth doesn't mind us cutting her sheet up!" Mandy shouted after him.

Mandy and Lucy laid the plastic sheet out on the ground, well away from Honey, and waited for William to come back with the scissors. PC Greenall helped them to cut off a narrow strip, and they laid it out on the grass.

"Should we lead Honey or ride her?" Lucy asked PC Greenall.

"I think you should lead her to start with, just in case she rears or shies away," the policeman replied. "And one of you could stand at the other side of the strip with the apple."

"I'll lead Honey," said Lucy, giving William the apples. Then she looked shyly at PC Greenall. "Maybe Marlow could do it first," she suggested. "Then Honey would see that there's nothing to worry about."

"That's a very good idea," the policeman agreed.

They watched as PC Greenall mounted Marlow again and walked towards the plastic strip. Marlow was very calm indeed. He stepped neatly over the plastic and stopped on the other side, looking as if there was nothing at all to be worried about. Mandy noticed that Honey was watching with a very interested expression on her gentle face.

"Now it's our turn, Honey," Lucy whispered.

Mandy watched, her heart in her mouth, as Lucy led Honey over to the plastic strip. William was already waiting at the other side, apple in hand. Lucy set off, keeping a careful eye on Honey. The pony looked a bit nervous, but this time she did not try to pull away. Instead she eyed the apple hungrily and followed Lucy across the strip towards William. A few seconds later, she was on the other side, crunching down the apple.

Mandy sighed with relief. Honey had done it!

"Oh, well done, Honey!" cried Lucy, flinging her arms around the pony's neck. "And well done, Marlow," she added, giving the big horse a piece of apple too. "This is all because of you."

"I don't think you'll have any problems now," PC Greenall beamed, sliding off Marlow and looping the reins over his arm. "As long as you take it easy, and don't try to do too much too soon. Don't make the strips wider too quickly. Give Honey plenty of time to get used to each one."

With PC Greenall and Marlow watching, Lucy led Honey backwards and forwards over the plastic strip several times without any problems at all. Mandy was thrilled. It looked like the Handy Pony training was back on track!

"Can we try riding Honey across now?" asked William.

PC Greenall nodded. "Just take it slowly," he advised. Then he looked surprised as William went over to Honey. "I thought *Lucy* was riding in the Handy Pony event?" he said.

Lucy turned bright red. So did William. No one knew what to say. Mandy realized she hadn't told PC Greenall that Lucy didn't ride Honey.

Lucy buried her face in Honey's neck, looking very embarrassed. "I'm scared of riding," she mumbled. "I fell off a pony a few months ago, and I haven't ridden since."

There was silence for a moment.

"Well, I can see that you're certainly not scared of horses," PC Greenall said gently. "Marlow's a very big horse, and you're not frightened of *him*."

"Oh no!" said Lucy, stroking the police horse's neck. "I could never be frightened of Marlow. He's lovely."

"You know, that advice I gave you about starting small and building up doesn't just work for horses," PC Greenall went on. "It works for people too."

"What do you mean?" asked Lucy.

"Well, there's no reason why you should get back on a horse and ride straight away," PC Greenall explained. "You could start off by just sitting on Honey. Then, when you feel comfortable, you could walk a little way. And then you could try trotting, and so on."

Mandy thought that sounded like a brilliant idea. She glanced at Lucy, who was looking over at Honey.

"I *think* I could sit on Honey's back," Lucy said in a shaky voice. "As long as I didn't have to go anywhere."

"That sounds very sensible," PC Greenall said kindly. "If you really want to." Beside him, Marlow snorted and tossed his head, as if he agreed.

Lucy nodded, and walked over to the pony. Mandy held her breath. She could see that

Lucy was trembling with nerves, but she also looked very determined.

Lucy carefully tightened Honey's girth. Then she took a deep breath and put her foot in the stirrup. She swung herself upwards and landed in the saddle. She looked down at Mandy and the others with a shaky smile.

"Lucy, you did it!" Mandy gasped, relief flooding through her. "Well done!"

William grinned broadly, and PC Greenall looked very pleased too.

"I can't believe it!" said Lucy, her eyes shining. "Thanks, PC Greenall, and thanks, Marlow. I couldn't have done this without you."

Mandy couldn't stop smiling. Maybe Lucy and Honey would be taking part in the Handy Pony competition after all!

9

Well done, Honey!

"It's only a few days to the Pony Club Show now, Mandy," said Mr Hope, as they climbed into the Land-rover. "How's Honey getting on?"

It was the following Wednesday after school, and Mr Hope was giving Mandy a lift to the stables. She had promised to meet Lucy and William there.

"She's doing just fine, Dad," Mandy answered eagerly. "PC Greenall and Marlow really helped us when they turned up last Saturday."

"And is Honey walking over a full-sized plastic sheet now?" asked Mandy's dad, as they drove through Welford.

Mandy shook her head. "Not *quite*," she said. "But we're not far off. I think Lucy is going to try it today."

"Well, good luck," said Mr Hope. "By the way, how's Lucy getting on? Has she started riding yet?"

"Not yet," Mandy admitted. "But she's been sitting on Honey every day. So that's a good sign."

"Let's hope so," said Mandy's dad, steering the Land-rover into the stable yard.

Mandy kissed her dad goodbye and jumped out of the car. She glanced across at the paddock. Lucy was already there with Honey, but there was no sign of William.

Mandy picked her way carefully through the stable yard, which was full of puddles of soapy water. She remembered that Lucy and William had been planning to give Honey a bath before the show on Saturday. Maybe that was where all the water had come from.

Mandy went over to the gate. She was about to call out to Lucy when she stopped. A plastic sheet was spread out in the middle of the field. Mandy could see that it was a full-sized sheet, not one that had been cut up into smaller strips. Lucy was leading Honey towards it. Mandy's heart began to thump. Would Honey make it this time, after all the help PC Greenall and Marlow had given her?

Mandy climbed quietly up on to the gate so that she could get a better view. Lucy and Honey didn't notice her as they walked slowly towards the sheet. Mandy could see that Lucy was talking quietly in her pony's ear, but this time Honey didn't seem scared at all as they stepped on to the plastic. She walked calmly beside Lucy, right across the sheet and on to the grass on the other side.

Mandy let out a loud cheer.

Lucy spotted her sitting on the gate and waved. "Did you see that?" she called. "Wasn't Honey great?"

"She's just as good as Marlow!" Mandy called back. She climbed down and ran over to them.

"Yes." Lucy looked proudly at her pony. "I think she might do quite well in the Handy Pony class."

That sounded as if Lucy was definitely thinking of riding at the show, Mandy thought hopefully. "Where's William?" she asked.

"He's gone to Walton with Mum to buy some new riding boots," said Lucy, smoothing Honey's silky mane with her fingers. "They dropped me off here first, and I gave Honey a bath. Doesn't she look nice?"

"She looks lovely," Mandy agreed, patting Honey's shining neck.

"They're coming back later to pick us up," Lucy went on. "William's going to be really pleased when I tell him what Honey's done."

"What do you want to do now?" Mandy asked. "Shall we practise some more of the Handy Pony things?"

"Well, I thought I might try sitting on Honey again," Lucy replied. "If you don't mind. I know it's a bit boring."

"No, that's a good idea," Mandy told her.

Lucy put her foot in the stirrup and pulled herself into the saddle. She was much less nervous about doing that now, even though she hadn't actually ridden any distance. Meanwhile, Mandy lay down on the grass, enjoying the feel of the sun on her face. The summer holidays were nearly here, she thought drowsily, and she was really looking forward to them. There were lots of things going on too. There was the Welford Show, and the County and Agricultural Show, as well as the Seven Dales Dog Show. And Gran and Grandad had promised to take her to the seaside for the day. It was going to be a *brilliant* summer holiday, Mandy decided dreamily.

Suddenly Mandy heard a noise that made her sit up. Her eyes opened very wide when she saw what was happening. Honey was walking slowly around the paddock with Lucy on her back. Lucy was *riding* Honey!

Mandy gasped. She had to clap her hand over her mouth to stop herself from calling out. She didn't want to distract Lucy or make Honey jump.

Lucy was sitting rather stiffly on Honey's back, clinging tightly to the reins. Her face was very pale. But soon she began to sit up taller and straighter, and look more comfortable.

She caught Mandy's eye and managed a smile. "I'm doing it all wrong!" she called.

"You're doing brilliantly!" Mandy called back.

Mandy watched closely as Lucy and Honey circled the field again. Honey was wonderful, Mandy thought. She seemed to understand that Lucy was feeling nervous, and was walking extra gently. Soon Lucy looked just like her old self.

"How are you feeling?" Mandy called.

"My knees are shaking, but I feel great!"

Lucy beamed. "I can't believe I was so scared. I've really missed riding."

To Mandy's delight, Lucy urged Honey into a trot, and then they cantered across the field. Lucy just couldn't stop smiling, and Mandy had to laugh when she saw the look on her friend's face.

"I think I've done enough for today," Lucy said breathlessly, reining Honey to a halt. "But now that I've started riding again, I don't want to stop!"

"William's going to get a big surprise when he arrives later on," Mandy said, going over to open the gate. "Do you think you'll be taking part in the Pony Club Show now?"

"Just try and stop me!" Lucy laughed. She rode Honey slowly through the gate and they headed towards the stable yard.

Mandy stayed behind to close the gate, letting Lucy and Honey go on ahead. Suddenly she remembered the puddles of water all over the yard. What would Honey do when she saw them? She wondered if she should call out to warn Lucy, but she didn't want to startle Honey. She ran over to the yard as fast as she could.

But Mandy was too late. Honey was already walking into the stable yard. And Lucy had spotted the puddles herself.

"Easy, Honey," she was murmuring. "Just take it nice and slowly. Come on now, keep going."

Mandy stood and watched as Honey moved forward. There was a puddle right ahead of her, but Honey didn't stop. She walked straight on through the puddle, sending up splashes of soapy water. Then they carried on through two more puddles, before Lucy drew her to a halt.

"Good girl, Honey," she said, patting the pony's neck.

Mandy hurried over. "I was really worried when I remembered all those puddles!" she burst out. "But you did brilliantly, Lucy."

"I just knew Honey would be OK," Lucy explained. "She did so well on the plastic sheet, I was sure she'd be all right with *real* puddles too."

Mandy nodded. "Here's your mum and William," she added, as a car pulled off the road and into the stables. "They're going to be so pleased!"

Lucy grinned. "Let's go and surprise them, shall we?" she laughed.

10

Marlow to the rescue

"I hope it's not still raining," Mandy muttered anxiously as she jumped out of bed.

It was Saturday morning, the day of the Welford Show. The night before, it had started to rain very heavily. It had still been raining when Mandy had gone to bed, and it had been quite windy too. Mandy frowned. She could still hear the wind whistling around the cottage. It sounded as if it had got even stronger.

She rushed over to the window, pulled back the curtains, and peered outside. To her relief, the rain had stopped. Although the sky was cloudy, she could see the sun trying to break through. But it was a lot more windy, and the trees were swaying to and fro.

"Oh no," Mandy said to herself. She hoped it would clear up before the show.

She got dressed quickly, and ran downstairs. Her mum and dad were already having breakfast.

"I hope you're not thinking of wearing a hat today, Mandy," her dad teased her. "Because I think it would blow away in about five seconds flat!"

"It *is* windy, isn't it?" remarked Mrs Hope, pouring Mandy a glass of juice. "Some of the ponies in the show won't like that at all."

"I think Honey will be all right," Mandy said, sliding into her chair.

"And we're so pleased that Lucy's going to be riding her," Mrs Hope added with a smile. "We can't wait to see the Handy Pony event."

"I think Lucy and Honey are going to do

really well," Mandy said. "They might even win."

"Well, we'll keep our fingers crossed." Mr Hope glanced at the clock. "I'd better get a move on. Morning surgery starts in five minutes."

Mandy began to eat her cereal. She'd cross *all* her fingers and toes if it helped Lucy and Honey to win the Handy Pony class. And it would be nice if William did well in the Junior Jumping too.

The Welford Show didn't start until eleven o'clock, and Mandy was on tenterhooks all morning, keeping an eye on the weather. Although the sun did manage to break through the clouds every so often, it was still very windy. By the time Mandy and her parents left to drive to the showground, the wind had whipped up even more.

"At least it's not raining," Mandy remarked, as they headed towards Farmer Redpath's field, where the show was held.

"I wonder who's opening it this year," said Mrs Hope. The show was always opened by a local celebrity. "Have you heard anything about it, Adam?"

"No, they've kept it pretty quiet this year." Mr Hope frowned.

"It's not you, is it, Dad?" Mandy grinned. "You're a local celebrity."

"Thank you, Mandy!" Her dad laughed. "No, it's not me. We'll just have to wait and see."

When they reached the field, Mandy looked round eagerly. There were people milling around everywhere, gathering for the grand opening. At one end of the field, three large rings had been set up for the Pony Club classes. As they drove towards the car parking area, Mandy noticed a huge silver horsebox. She wondered who it belonged to. It looked far too big for any of the Pony Club ponies.

As usual, there were lots of tents and stalls dotted around the field, as well as a big marquee for refreshments. The tents were flapping madly in the breeze, and so was the brightly-coloured bunting which hung from the trees. It was making quite a noise. Mandy wondered if the horses and ponies would mind.

Then she spotted her friend Paul Stevens. He was leading his Exmoor pony, Paddy, past the marquee, when there was a really strong gust of wind. The canvas sides of the marquee flapped loudly, and Paddy shied away, looking rather scared. Paul had to hang on to the pony's reins and calm him down before they could walk on.

"Oh dear," Mandy said to her mum. "I bet a lot of the ponies are going to be frightened, just like Paddy."

"Mandy!" Lucy was running towards her, waving madly. William was behind her. "We've been looking for you."

"We've only just arrived," Mandy explained. "Where's Honey?"

"She's by the collecting ring," said William.

"But we don't want to leave her for too long," Lucy went on. "My mum and dad are with her at the moment."

"I think it's time for the official opening," said Mr Hope, glancing at the stage that had been set up in the middle of the field. Mrs Ponsonby, who was the chairperson of the show committee, was fussing around as usual. There were other people on the platform too, including Miss Fletcher and Mrs Forsyth.

"Ladies and gentlemen," began Mrs Ponsonby loudly, with one hand clutching

her enormous flowery hat. "Once again, welcome to the Welford Show. Before we have our official opening, I would like to hand over to Mrs Forsyth from our local stables, who will explain just where the money we raise is going this year."

Mrs Forsyth stood up. "I am pleased to tell you that the money from this year's show will go to help care for retired police horses," she said. "Our police horses do a fine job, and I know you will all agree that this is a very worthy cause."

There was loud applause. Mandy, Lucy and

William clapped as hard as they could.

"And now I can see our guest of honour coming towards us," Mrs Forsyth went on. "Please give a warm welcome to PC Greenall and Marlow!"

"Oh!" Mandy gasped, spinning round to see the policeman leading Marlow across the grass towards the stage. "So *that* was why PC Greenall was at the stables last week, to see Mrs Forsyth about the show."

"William, that huge horsebox we saw must have been Marlow's," Lucy said breathlessly, her eyes shining. "We wondered who it belonged to."

There was more applause as PC Greenall faced the crowd, with Marlow standing quietly next to him. PC Greenall was wearing his police uniform and looked very smart. Marlow looked very well-groomed too, Mandy thought admiringly. His coat shone and his tack gleamed.

"PC Greenall and Marlow will also be presenting today's winners with their rosettes," Mrs Forsyth added. "Now over to you, PC Greenall."

"Well, Marlow and I are very pleased to be

here," PC Greenall began. "Especially as you've so kindly agreed to donate all the money raised today to our retired police horse charity. Please enjoy yourselves, and spend as much as you can!"

Everyone laughed.

"I now declare the Welford Show open," PC Greenall announced, and everyone laughed again as Marlow whinnied in agreement.

"Isn't it great that Marlow's here?" Lucy said happily, as Miss Fletcher led PC Greenall and the police horse across the field to the Pony Club rings. "Look, I think they're coming to watch our events."

"I'd better go," said William. "Junior Jumping is the first class in Ring One."

"Mum, can we go and watch William and Honey?" Mandy asked, and her parents nodded.

"I'll come too," Lucy said. "The Handy Pony is the third class in Ring Three, so I've got plenty of time. And it means that Honey can have a rest in between her classes."

They all went over to Ring One. Mandy spotted Honey waiting patiently in the collecting area with Mr and Mrs Kaye. She looked spotlessly clean, and very calm. The flapping tents didn't seem to bother her at all.

Meanwhile, Miss Fletcher and Mrs Forsyth were sitting at a table near the rings with PC Greenall. Marlow stood patiently next to them, beside a big oak tree. On the table in front of them was a large box containing the winners' rosettes.

"Let's go and say hello to Marlow and PC Greenall," Mandy suggested. "We've got a few minutes before the Junior Jumping starts."

"Oh, yes," Lucy said eagerly. "I want to tell him that I've started riding again."

Mandy and Lucy headed over to the table, but before they reached it, something dreadful happened. A heavy gust of wind caught the box of rosettes and tipped it over. Miss Fletcher tried to grab it, but she was too late. All of the rosettes flew out of the box, and the wind swirled them upwards. They fluttered into the air like brightly-coloured birds. The rosettes, which were quite heavy, fell to the ground again, but the champion's gold sash lodged itself firmly in the tree overhead.

"Oh no!" Mandy gasped, running over to the table. Lucy followed her. Everyone sitting around the rings was looking and pointing, too.

"Oh dear." Miss Fletcher stared helplessly up at the sash in the tree. "What *are* we going to do?"

"We can't start the events until we get the sash down," Mrs Forsyth frowned. "It would be too distracting for the ponies and their riders."

Miss Fletcher looked very upset. "But we have to start on time," she said. "We've so much to get through."

"Maybe we can find a stepladder," PC Greenall suggested.

"Yes, there must be one around somewhere," agreed Miss Fletcher, and hurried away.

Mandy wondered anxiously how long it would take Miss Fletcher to find a stepladder. Surely there must be a quicker way?

Suddenly she had an idea. "Maybe someone could stand on Marlow's back and get the sash down," she said. "Marlow's just as strong as a stepladder!"

PC Greenall nodded slowly. "It would have

to be someone tall," he said, "but they'd have to be light, too. An adult would be too heavy."

"I don't think I'm tall enough," Mandy said. She glanced around the field. There must be somebody who could do it.

"I'm tall, and I'm not very heavy," Lucy said, sounding very excited. "Let me have a go."

PC Greenall looked hard at her. "Are you sure?" he asked.

"Yes, I'm sure," Lucy said firmly. "I've started riding again," she added.

PC Greenall looked pleased. "That's great news," he said. "Let's see what we can do about getting this champion's sash back, then."

He led Marlow over to the tree, and Mandy held the horse's reins while Lucy climbed on. PC Greenall gave her a hand, because Marlow was so big. The ringside audience watched, fascinated.

"Take it slowly, Lucy," PC Greenall warned.

Mandy watched anxiously as Lucy pulled herself upright. She wobbled a bit as she was standing up, but soon she was able to reach the lower branches of the tree and hold on to them. Lucy had to stand on tiptoe to reach the champion's sash, which was caught on a

branch, but she managed to untangle it. Marlow didn't move at all. He stood there solidly, as still as stone.

"Someone's gone to look for a stepladder," Miss Fletcher announced, as she hurried back. Then she saw Lucy standing on Marlow's back. "Oh!"

"I don't think we need one now, Miss Fletcher," Mandy laughed, handing over the sash.

There was loud applause as Lucy scrambled carefully down from Marlow's back with PC Greenall's help.

"Thank you, Lucy," Miss Fletcher said gratefully. "Now we really must start the first events."

Lucy and Mandy hurried over to Ring One and joined Mandy's mum and dad, who were sitting with Mr and Mrs Kaye.

"Looks like you're quite a heroine, Lucy," Mr Hope said with a smile.

"Yes, well done, dear," said Mrs Kaye, giving Lucy a hug. "You were very brave."

"No, I wasn't," said Lucy, turning pink. "It was easy because Marlow was so brilliant. He stood really still."

"Look, the Junior Jumping's about to start," Mandy said. "Here comes the first entrant."

"When is it William's turn?" asked Mr Kaye, studying his programme.

"I think he's third, Dad," replied Lucy.

The Junior Jumping contest began. Mandy realized that she had been right when she thought a lot of the ponies would be scared by the wind. Both of the first two ponies were spooked by the bunting flapping in the trees, and one refused to jump at all. Then it was William and Honey's turn. Mandy held her breath, but Honey was as calm as could be. The flapping tents and the flags didn't bother her one bit as she trotted happily round the ring.

"Isn't Honey great?" Lucy said proudly.

The bell rang to signal the start of William's round. He did very well, but they didn't quite manage a clear round. They knocked one jump down, and when the results were announced at the end, William and Honey had come third. William looked a bit disappointed at not winning, but he soon cheered up when both Mrs Forsyth and Miss Fletcher told him that he'd done very well for a beginner.

Mandy and her parents went off to look round the rest of the show after that, but Mandy kept a sharp eye on the clock. Ten minutes before the Handy Pony event was due to start, the Hopes hurried back to Ring Three, and joined Mr and Mrs Kaye and William to watch Lucy and Honey.

Mandy was so excited, she could hardly sit still. But luckily she didn't have to wait long, because Lucy and Honey were first into the ring. Mandy clapped really hard, and then sat forward eagerly to watch.

Honey and Lucy began by walking through a narrow corridor of straw bales. Then came weaving in and out of poles, walking under a line of washing, Round the World and walking past two people blowing whistles and shouting loudly. Mandy got more and more excited as Lucy and Honey performed everything smoothly without collecting any penalty points at all.

Then it was time for Honey to walk across the plastic sheet. Even though Mandy knew that Honey had overcome her fear of puddles now, she couldn't help feeling a bit nervous. But Honey didn't put a foot wrong.

She crossed the plastic sheet without any sign of nerves. Lucy didn't look worried either.

Hardly daring to breathe, Mandy watched Honey and Lucy complete the last few tasks. When Lucy had rung the bell and replaced it carefully on the barrel, it was all over. Lucy and Honey had completed the Handy Pony in good time, without a single penalty point. The Hopes and the Kayes cheered and clapped loudly.

"Lucy and Honey have really set a challenge for the rest of the Handy Pony entrants!" Miss Fletcher announced over the tannoy. "Well done. Next we have Mark Poole on Sunset."

Mandy felt excitement bubbling up inside her as, one by one, the Handy Pony competitors came into the ring. No one managed a clear round except for Honey and Lucy. In fact, a few of the ponies were very upset by the strong wind, even though they were supposed to ignore loud noises. One bolted right out of the ring. By the end of the event only one pony had no penalty points at all.

"And the winner of the Handy Pony class

is Lucy Kaye on Honey!" Miss Fletcher announced.

Mandy and William leaped to their feet, cheering loudly.

Lucy looked totally thrilled. She rushed over to them, leading Honey alongside her. "We did it!" she gasped. "Thanks for all your help, Mandy. We couldn't have done it without you."

"I didn't do much." Mandy grinned. "I think you ought to thank Marlow and PC Greenall too!"

"Oh, I will!" Lucy said, beaming all over her face.

They looked over at PC Greenall, who grinned at Lucy and gave her a thumbs–up sign.

"First prize in the Handy Pony class goes to Lucy Kaye and Honey!" declared Miss Fletcher from the platform.

Mandy clapped until her hands hurt, as Lucy and Honey stepped forward to receive their red rosette from PC Greenall and Marlow. PC Greenall shook Lucy's hand, then pinned the rosette to Honey's bridle. Mandy saw

Lucy talking earnestly to the policeman and patting Marlow, and she guessed that Lucy was thanking them. Then Mrs Forsyth stepped forward and whispered something in Lucy's ear. Lucy looked very surprised, and nodded. Mandy wondered what Mrs Forsyth had said to her.

When all the rosettes had been handed out, Mrs Forsyth stood up again. "Very well done to all our winners," she said. "And now we have our most important prize to present." She picked up the champion's sash from the table. "And you may be surprised to hear that I'm not going to ask PC Greenall and Marlow to present this one!"

Mandy wondered what on earth was going on. PC Greenall looked just as surprised as everyone else.

"Instead, I'm going to ask Lucy Kaye to present this sash to this year's champion horse," Mrs Forsyth went on with a smile.

The audience clapped as Lucy stepped forward, looking rather pink. "This year's champion's sash is presented to the horse who saved the day," she said, raising her voice so that everyone could hear. "Without him, we wouldn't have had any prizes today. The champion's sash goes to Marlow. He's a real horse hero!"

"Oh!" Mandy gasped with delight.

There was a loud cheer as PC Greenall led Marlow towards Lucy, and helped her to put the champion's sash round Marlow's neck.

Mandy grinned happily. Everything had turned out brilliantly in the end, thanks to PC Greenall and Marlow.

RAT RIDDLE
Animal Ark Pets 18

Lucy Daniels

Mandy and James's school-friend Martin
has been given a pair of fancy rats for his
birthday. Cheddar and Pickle love to race
around their 'Incredible Rat Run'. At
first, Mandy finds that Pickle is the fastest.
But then Pickle's times begin to slow
down. Could something be wrong?

FOAL FROLICS
Animal Ark Pets Summer Special

Lucy Daniels

Mandy and James are on holiday with Mandy's family. All sorts of things are disappearing from the campsite, and now golf balls from the nearby golf course are going missing too. It's a mystery until Mandy and James catch the thief red-handed: a cheeky foal called Mischief! The bad-tempered groundsman at the golf course wants Mischief removed. Can Mandy and James find a way for the foal to stay?

CALF CAPERS
Animal Ark Pets Summer Shows Trilogy 2

Lucy Daniels

Mandy is keen to see Tilly the Dexter calf win a prize at the Welford County Show. But strange things keep happening to Tilly and her mum, Jenny. It looks like someone doesn't want them to take part in the show at all. Mandy and James are determined to find out what is going on!

Another Hodder Children's book

PUPPY PRIZES
Animal Ark Pets Summer Shows Trilogy 3

Lucy Daniels

The Seven Dales Dog Show is coming to Welford! James is entering with Blackie, and so is their friend Max with his Cairn terrier, Sandy. Best of all, Mandy is taking part with Mrs Trigg's dog, Holly! Will any of the pups come home with a prize?

LUCY DANIELS

Animal Ark Pets

0 340 67283 8	Puppy Puzzle	£3.99	☐
0 340 67284 6	Kitten Crowd	£3.99	☐
0 340 67285 4	Rabbit Race	£3.99	☐
0 340 67286 2	Hamster Hotel	£3.99	☐
0 340 68729 0	Mouse Magic	£3.99	☐
0 340 68730 4	Chick Challenge	£3.99	☐
0 340 68731 2	Pony Parade	£3.99	☐
0 340 68732 0	Guinea-pig Gang	£3.99	☐
0 340 71371 2	Gerbil Genius	£3.99	☐
0 340 71372 0	Duckling Diary	£3.99	☐
0 340 71373 9	Lamb Lessons	£3.99	☐
0 340 71374 7	Doggy Dare	£3.99	☐
0 340 73585 6	Donkey Derby	£3.99	☐
0 340 73586 4	Hedgehog Home	£3.99	☐
0 340 73587 2	Frog Friends	£3.99	☐
0 340 73588 0	Bunny Bonanza	£3.99	☐
0 340 73589 9	Ferret Fun	£3.99	☐
0 340 73590 2	Rat Riddle	£3.99	☐
0 340 73592 9	Cat Crazy	£3.99	☐
0 340 73605 4	Pets' Party	£3.99	☐
0 340 73593 7	Foal Frolics	£3.99	☐
0 340 77861 X	Piglet Pranks	£3.99	☐
0 340 77878 4	Spaniel Surprise	£3.99	☐
0 340 85204 6	Horse Hero	£3.99	☐
0 340 85205 4	Calf Capers	£3.99	☐
0 340 85206 2	Puppy Prizes	£3.99	☐

All Hodder Children's books are available at your local bookshop, or can be ordered direct from the publisher. Just tick the titles you would like and complete the details below. Prices and availability are subject to change without prior notice.

Please enclose a cheque or postal order made payable to *Bookpoint Ltd*, and send to: Hodder Children's Books, 39 Milton Park, Abingdon, OXON OX14 4TD, UK. Email Address: orders@bookpoint.co.uk

If you would prefer to pay by credit card, our call centre team would be delighted to take your order by telephone. Our direct line *01235 400414* (lines open 9.00 am–6.00 pm Monday to Saturday, 24 hour message answering service). Alternatively you can send a fax on *01235 400454*.

TITLE		FIRST NAME		SURNAME	

ADDRESS	
DAYTIME TEL:	POST CODE

If you would prefer to pay by credit card, please complete:
Please debit my Visa/Access/Diner's Card/American Express (delete as applicable) card no:

Signature .... Expiry Date: ....

If you would NOT like to receive further information on our products please tick the box. ☐